Eric's Elephant
Goes Camping

Eric's Elephant Goes Camping

John Gatehouse

Illustrated by
Sue Cony

PUFFIN BOOKS

PUFFIN BOOKS

Published by the Penguin Group
Penguin Books Ltd, 27 Wrights Lane, London W8 5TZ, England
Penguin Putnam Inc., 375 Hudson Street, New York, New York 10014, USA
Penguin Books Australia Ltd, Ringwood, Victoria, Australia
Penguin Books Canada Ltd, 10 Alcorn Avenue, Toronto, Ontario, Canada M4V 3B2
Penguin Books (NZ) Ltd, Private Bag 102902, NSMC, Auckland, New Zealand

Penguin Books Ltd, Registered Offices: Harmondsworth, Middlesex, England

First published by Hamish Hamilton Ltd 1996
Published in Puffin Books 1998
3 5 7 9 10 8 6 4

Text copyright © John Gatehouse, 1996
Illustrations copyright © Sue Cony, 1996
All rights reserved

Printed in Hong Kong by Midas Printing Limited

British Library Cataloguing in Publication Data
A CIP catalogue record for this book is available from the British Library

ISBN 0-140-38838-9

Eric owned a very unusual pet. It was a
real, live, white elephant that he had won
at the Church Jumble Sale.

One morning, Eric woke up feeling very
excited. He was going on a camping trip
with his dad. Eric had never been camping
before.

"Can I take my elephant with me?" he asked his mother as he brushed his teeth.

"No, you can't!" she said. "That elephant causes nothing but trouble. She stays RIGHT HERE in the garden shed!"

Eric was very disappointed.

So was his elephant.

"Don't worry," said Eric, patting her on the trunk. "I'll only be gone one night." And he waved her goodbye.

Eric's elephant watched sadly as Eric's dad packed the tent inside the car.

"I'm glad your elephant isn't coming with us," he muttered, as Eric clambered into the passenger seat and put on his seatbelt. "I wouldn't have a moment's peace with her along."

Eric's elephant waited until Eric and his dad had driven away, and Eric's mum had gone inside to clean the house. Then she pulled hard on the rope that tethered her to the shed.

The shed moved . . . just a little bit.

Eric's elephant pulled HARDER. The shed moved again.

She dragged the shed along the garden, across Eric's dad's prize flower patch and *through* the garden fence.

CRRRAAAASSSH!!

She set off towards the forest . . .

By the time Eric and his dad had set up
the tent and had enjoyed a hearty meal, it
was growing dark. They snuggled up
around the camp fire and Eric's dad told
him a spooky story.

"Oooh!" giggled Eric, excitedly. "I hope there are no ghosts in *this* forest!"

"Don't be silly, Eric," said his dad. "There are no such things as ghosts!"

Suddenly there was a loud rustling in the bushes. It grew LOUDER and LOUDER!

A pair of big yellow eyes appeared from out of the darkness!

"Waaaaaaah! I-I-It's a G-G-G-GHOST!!"
screamed Eric's dad, scrambling up a tree.

Eric's elephant appeared from behind the
bushes, dragging the shed behind her.

"No, it's not!" cheered Eric. "It's my
elephant!"

Eric's dad was not amused.

"Humph! Well, we can't take her back home now!" he muttered, sliding back down the tree. "She'll have to stay here, with us."

"Yippee!" cheered Eric.

"TOOT! TOOT!" trumpeted his
elephant.

Eric untied his elephant from the shed.
"Mum told you to stay in the shed," he
chuckled. "And you did!"

That night, Eric's elephant slept in her shed. But the hooting of the owls frightened her. So she sneaked into the tent instead.

"Hey, gerroff!" shouted Eric's dad, as she tried to squeeze inside his sleeping bag. "This is *our* tent! GO AWAY!"

Eric's elephant rolled over . . . and the tent came crashing down!

"You big lump!" bellowed Eric's dad. "You've wrecked our tent! Now we have nowhere to sleep!"

Eric and his dad had to sleep with the elephant in *her* shed. It was a tight fit.

The next morning, Eric and his dad went down to the stream to wash themselves. Eric's elephant went with them.

Eric's dad splashed his face with cold water. Eric did the same.

Eric's elephant thought they were playing
a game. She filled up her trunk with water
and squirted it all over Eric's dad!
SPLOOOOSSSSH!

"Waaaaah!" he squealed, falling
backwards into the stream. "I wanted to
wash my face – not *all* of me!"

"Oh dear!" sighed Eric, leading his
elephant away. "Dad's going bonkers
again. We had better hide until he calms
down."

Eric's elephant wasn't listening. She could smell food . . . and she was feeling VERY HUNGRY.

"Hey! Slow down, you big lump!" cried Eric, as his elephant dashed away, dragging him through a prickly hedge. "Where are you going?"

PC Crumble, Mrs Groggins and Mr Sprout were also camping in the forest. They were enjoying a nice, quiet breakfast.

"And there are no elephants to disturb us!" chuckled Mrs Groggins, who had had trouble with Eric's elephant before. So had PC Crumble and Mr Sprout.

"Funny you should say that," said Eric, as his elephant burst out from behind the bushes. But PC Crumble, Mrs Groggins and Mr Sprout did not laugh.

They were too busy watching Eric's elephant as she sucked up their breakfast in her trunk and pushed it into her mouth.

"Oh dear!" groaned Eric, as his elephant ran off, chased by Eric, PC Crumble, Mrs Groggins and Mr Sprout. "Can't you do anything right? Now *everyone* is going bonkers!"

Eric's elephant wasn't listening . . . nor was she looking where she was going. She collided with a man who was coming out of a wooden shack carrying a big, bulging sack. The man toppled backwards, turning somersaults on the ground until his head became stuck in a rabbit hole.

"Not again!" groaned Eric. "We could get thrown into jail for this!"

PC Crumble caught up with Eric and his elephant. He looked at the man whose head was stuck in the rabbit hole. Then he looked inside the big, bulging sack on the ground. It was filled with lots and lots of money!

"Well done!" he said, patting Eric's elephant on the trunk. "You've caught Big Ben, the bank robber. I've been after him for ages! He must have been hiding out in this forest."

"Coo!" gasped Eric, as his elephant wrapped her trunk around Big Ben's legs and pulled him out of the rabbit hole. "We might get a reward for this."

A police van came to collect Big Ben. All the policemen cheered Eric's elephant. Eric felt very proud.

Eric used the reward money to buy a new tent for his dad. And a new fence. And lots and lots of new flowers for the garden.

"Can we go camping again?" Eric asked his dad, after they had returned home.

"Not likely!" said his dad. "I'm never going to go camping with that elephant again!"

So Eric and his elephant went camping by themselves . . . in the back garden.

"Now we can go camping whenever we like!" chuckled Eric, peeking out from his tent.

"TOOT! TOOT!" agreed Eric's elephant from her shed. She thought camping was LOTS of fun!